Hooray for School!
Going to School with

by Brooke Lindner
illustrated by Susan Hall

SCHOLASTIC INC.
New York Toronto London Auckland Sydney
Mexico City New Delhi Hong Kong Buenos Aires

ISBN-13: 978-0-545-07728-6
ISBN-10: 0-545-07728-1

12 11 10 9 8 7 6 5 4 3 2 1   8 9 10 11 12 13/0

Printed in the U.S.A.

First Scholastic printing, September 2008

Tomorrow is the first day of school!
There are so many great things to
do at school.

I can't wait for school to start!
I love using the school computer.
It's just like the one I have in the
Animal Rescue Center! What do
you like to do on the computer?

I love learning new things in school. Do you know what my favorite class is? I'll give you a hint! *Uno, dos, tres, cuatro, cinco, seis, siete, ocho, nueve, diez. ¡Sí!* My favorite subject is math! What's your favorite subject?

I love seeing all of my friends at school. And I love feeding our class pet, Giggles the rabbit. What class pet would you like to have?

I like to visit the school library. I can find a lot of books about animal science there. The more I read about animals, the better I am at being an Animal Rescuer!

One of my favorite parts of school is recess! I love to play games with my friends. What are your favorite games to play at recess?

There's something else that I really love to do at school! Here's a clue: A, B, C. Yeah, I love writing letters and words, and making stories. Sometimes I even get to share my stories in class!

I can't wait for tomorrow to come!
Now it's time to go to sleep so I'll
be ready for my big day at school.
¡Buenas noches! Good night!

Rise and shine! It's almost time for school. Let's pack some lunch. What are your favorite foods to bring to school?

Let's check Backpack to make sure I have everything I need for school. Backpack has crayons, pencils, a notebook, a ruler, and my lunch. *¡Excelente!*

¡Vamos a la escuela!
Let's go to school!

Have a great day!